3 FOLKTALES FROM EASTERN EUROPE AND CENTRAL ASIA

Stories from the Ukraine, Latvia, and Turkmen

by Gini Graham Scott, Ph.D.

3 FOLKTALES FROM EASTERN EUROPE AND CENTRAL ASIA

TABLE OF CONTENTS

INTRODUCTION

The following three tales are adapted from stories told by the peasants in Eastern Europe and Central Asia. They are drawn from some books I found in shops when I visited the former U.S.S.R. in 1988 as part of a citizens diplomacy group.

I was intrigued by these folktales, since my paternal grandmother lived for some time in Odessa in the Ukraine, and I found they share a common theme – the poor peasant is able to succeed despite obstacles against an unfair ruler. He does so by being wise or generous and having a strong desire to help and protect his family, while the powerful ruler or rich merchant is foiled by his own greed. These are themes which resonate today, when inequality and social justice have become central issues of our times.

The following stories from Eastern Europe come from the Ukraine, Latvia, and Turkmen. These are three of my favorite stories.

THE LORD OF THE CROWS

An Adaptation of a Traditional Folktale from the Ukraine

Sasha lived on a farm with his parents, two older brothers, and three sisters in a small hut in the Ukrainian countryside. Though his father worked hard, the family was very poor. Their plot of land was too small for a good harvest, and his father only owned two thin oxen, so often they had little to eat.

In the spring, Sasha helped his father plow the field. As his father guided the oxen, he tossed seeds in the furrows.

One day, the sunny sky grew dark and Sasha saw a huge black bird circling above. Its sharp beak was like a sword, its long claws like hooks. When the bird landed, its outstretched wings covered Sasha, his father, and the oxen.

"I am the Lord of the Crows," he announced in a loud, gravely voice to Sasha's father. "I have come to get tribute for your land. What will you give me -- your son or your oxen? My children at home are hungry, and I want to feed them."

"No, no," Sasha's father pleaded. "Don't take my son or my oxen. Take me instead. My son is young and my family needs the oxen, so we can grow wheat and vegetables to eat."

The Lord of the Crows shook his head. "No. You are too old for a good meal. You must choose -- your son or your oxen."

He flapped his large wings and the earth trembled. The old man grabbed Sasha firmly.

"No. I cannot give up my son to such a fate. You may take my oxen."

"A good choice," the Lord of Crows replied. "Your oxen will make a much better meal for my children. So I will pay you well for your oxen."

As the crow grabbed the oxen and plow in his claws and rose into the air, the sun came out again.

"Just send one of your sons to my palace in the forest," he called out. "I will give him whatever he wants. It's a hard long journey, but someone he meets along the way can help him find my palace."

Then, the crow flew away.

When Sasha and his father returned home without the oxen, his mother burst into loud sobs.

"Oh, no. Now we can't plow and sow our seeds. So, surely we will starve."

Igor, the eldest son, spoke up to comfort her. "Don't cry, Mother. I'll go see the Lord of the Crows. Since he said he will pay for the oxen, I'll get the money to buy what we need."

The next day, Igor set off for the palace, holding a small loaf of bread his mother baked for him. On the way, he crossed two steep hills and a low valley. As he entered the forest, it grew darker and darker.

Soon he felt hungry and sat down on a log. As he took a bite of bread, a lame one-legged crow appeared on the path and hopped over to him.

"Hello," said the crow. "I'm very hungry. Can you give me a piece of your bread?"

Igor shook his head. "No. I have very little to eat and I'm hungry, too. I have a long way to go."

"I'm going through the forest, too," said the crow. "But my wings and legs are too weak to go any further. Can you carry me on your shoulder, and I'll show you the way?"

"No," said Igor. "I'm too tired myself, and you'll be too heavy."

Dejected, the crow flapped his wings and flew off, while Igor finished his bread.

Then, Igor walked fast to get to the palace more quickly. But night was falling, so soon he couldn't see the path and lost his way.

At home, Sasha and his parents, brothers, and sisters waited for Igor. But after a month, they gave up hope, and Sasha's next-oldest brother Boris told his mother: "I will find out what happened to Igor, and I will go to the Lord of the Crows' palace to get the money for the oxen."

The next day, Boris set off with a small loaf of bread from his mother. Like Igor, Boris crossed the two hills and low valley, then entered the deep forest. It became darker as he walked.

Feeling hungry and tired, he sat down by a bubbling stream and took his bread from his bag. But before he could take a bite, the lame old crow appeared through the trees and hopped over.

"Please," the crow begged. "I'm so hungry. Give me a piece of your bread."

Boris looked at the crow scornfully. "Why should I give you anything? Your Lord took away our oxen, so ask him to feed you."

The crow pleaded with him: "Can you at least carry me across the forest on your shoulder, since I am hungry and lame?"

"Why should I?" snapped Boris. "Ask the Lord of the Crows to help you."

So with a hop, the lame crow jumped across the stream and flew away.

After Boris finished his bread, he plunged deeper into the forest. But when night fell, he became confused in the dark, shadowy forest and soon lost his way.

After another month without either brother returning, Sasha announced: "I will go to the Lord of the Crows' palace to get the money. And I will try to find my brothers."

Though his mother and father pleaded with him, saying: "Don't go. You are our last son," Sasha insisted. "I must go, because I am the only one left to get the money and find my brothers."

The next day, he headed off with a small loaf of bread from his mother. After several days, he, too, was deep inside the forest. As it grew darker, he became very hungry and tired. When he sat down and took his first bite of bread, the lame crow limped over.

"Please, a piece of your bread," he begged. He hopped on one leg, flapped his wings weakly, and looked at Sasha with large pleading eyes.

Sasha gazed at the bird with pity. "You poor thing," he said. "Here's a piece of my bread. I have enough for two. Besides, I would enjoy your company after my long walk alone."

The crow sat down beside him and gobbled up the bread.

"Thank you so much," he said when he finished. "Now I have one more favor to ask. Can you give me a ride to the Lord of the Crows' palace?"

Sasha hesitated, since the crow looked so heavy.

"But I'm lame and my wings are weak," the crow pleaded.

So Sasha finally agreed. He lifted the crow onto his shoulder and headed down the path. When it grew dark, the crow whispered in his ear: "Let me show you the way or you will surely get lost."

As Sasha walked, the crow told him what to do: "Go right...Now left...Now straight ahead...Watch out for that hole, so you don't fall in."

Day after day, they traveled until they came to a grove bathed in sunlight.

Beyond it, Sasha saw a high cliff and on top was a large white palace with many towers.

"That's the palace," the lame crow said. "Now you can find your way alone. But before I leave, I want to give you some advice, since you were so kind to me." The crow leaned close and whispered in Sasha's ear. "The Lord of the Crows will ask what you want for the oxen. Tell him you only want what he puts under his pillow before he goes to bed at night."

Then, flapping his wings, the crow flew away.

Sasha walked on and climbed the steep path to the palace. Two black crows guarding the gate led him inside, and he followed them into a long room with silver walls. The Lord of the Crows sat on a high silver throne.

As Sasha walked over and bowed in greeting, the Lord of the Crows looked at him in amazement and asked: "How did you get here? No human has ever found his way here before."

"Oh, some kind people I met in the forest told me where to go," Sasha said, not wanting to tell about the lame crow.

The Lord of the Crows leaned back in his throne. "Well, since you are here, I must keep my promise to give you whatever you want for your oxen. Look around my palace and tell me what you want."

For the next three days, Sasha stayed as a guest. At night, he slept in a room with gold satin sheets, and each day, he walked from room to room, seeing the palace's many treasures. He saw chests of gold, silver jewelry, and fine silk clothes.

Then, he humbly knelt before the Lord of the Crows to tell him what he wanted.

"You have a beautiful palace. I liked many things. Yet my family and I don't need such riches. Instead, I will ask for only one thing. Just give me what you put under your pillow at night."

The Lord of the Crows grimaced in anger and beat his wings against his throne. He called for the guards at each door to come before him and yelled at them loudly. "How did the boy find out about this? Someone who showed him around the palace must have told him. Go find this crow and cut off his head."

As the guards flew off, the Lord of the Crows turned back to Sasha. "You must change your mind about what you want," he said angrily. "You must not ask for what you cannot have. Instead, I will reward you richly with a dozen oxen and a wagon full of gold."

Sasha thought about how much his father needed the oxen to plow and how much his mother would like the gold. Then, he recalled what the lame crow told him and replied: "No. I want only what you put under your pillow at night."

At last the Lord of the Crows agreed. "All right. Since you insist and I have given my word, you may have that."

He ordered a guard to fetch the object. Soon the guard returned holding a small copper coffee-grinder.

The Lord of the Crows shoved the grinder at Sasha. "Here. Take this and go away, before I go back on my word and have my guards peck you to death. I never want to see you again."

Terrified, Sasha put the grinder in his bag and fled from the place. Back in the forest, he sat down to rest. Hungrily, he reached into his bag for some bread. But none was left.

Sadly, he took out the grinder and looked at it closely. How ordinary it seemed, made of copper, not silver or gold.

"What a poor choice, I have made," Sasha said to himself. "I shouldn't have listened to that lame bird. I should have taken the oxen, gold, and a little food. Now I will surely starve and never get home."

Sasha held up the grinder and was about to throw it away in disgust, when he suddenly wondered: why did the Lord of the Crows offer him all his riches, if he didn't take this grinder?

He looked at the grinder more closely. Yet it still seemed like any other coffee grinder, with a wooden handle to one side.

Sasha sighed to himself. "I wish I had a table here with plenty to eat and drink, like the one in the palace."

As he put the grinder down, he gave the handle a little twist. At once, a table with a golden cloth, several bottles of wine, and large platter of chicken, potatoes, and cabbage appeared before him.

Sasha jumped up happily. "What wonderful things this grinder can do," he exclaimed.

Then, thinking of his family far away and his brothers lost in the forest, he was sad again.

I wish we were together again," he said to himself, again tapping the handle.

A moment later, his father, mother, brothers, and sisters were seated at the table with him, and they eagerly enjoyed the feast with him.

When they finished, Sasha wished they were all back home. An instant later, they were.

"Now I wish our home was larger and more comfortable," he said. At once it became twice as big and had white curtains and a thick brown rug.

Now Sasha and his family never lacked for anything they needed. Sasha only had to make a wish and twist the coffee-grinder's handle, and they soon had whatever they wanted.

As for the Lord of the Crows, he was so upset at the loss of his magic coffee grinder that he lost all his power and shrank in size. So now he is just another crow.

Sasha's father even shoos him away sometimes.

THE MAGIC RING

An Adaptation of a Traditional Folktale from Latvia

Vadim lived with his father in a small house in a village in Latvia. He helped his father plant and till the fields in the spring and helped with the fall harvest.

One summer morning, his father discovered the cupboards were almost bare. "Go to the market and buy some bread," he said, giving Vadim a few coins.

Vadim set off whistling a song on the path to the village.

Near the market, Vadim passed a peasant beating a dog with a large stick and went over to the peasant.

"Please, don't beat the dog," he begged. "I'll give you my coins if you let him go."

The peasant held up his stick and smiled. "Certainly. For your coins, I'll stop beating the dog."

He put down the stick and took the coins.

After Vadim returned home empty-handed, his father asked: "Where is the bread?"

Vadim didn't want to tell his father what he had done, so he simply said: "The coins you gave me weren't enough. I need more money."

And that night they had no bread to eat.

The following morning, Vadim's father again asked him to go to the market, saying: "Here are some more coins."

Again Vadim set off.

But along the way, he passed a peasant beating a mouse with a large rock. The mouse squeaked plaintively in pain.

Vadim felt sorry for the mouse and went over to the peasant. "Please, don't beat the mouse," he begged. "I'll give you my coins if you let him go."

The peasant held up his rock and smiled. "Certainly," he agreed.

He put down the rock and took the coins.

Again Vadim returned home without any food, explaining "I still need more money. The coins you gave me were not enough."

So Vadim and his father went hungry that night, too.

On the third morning, Vadim's father once more asked him to go to the market, telling him: "Be sure to buy the bread. There's nothing to eat in the house."

But this time, Vadim passed a peasant beating a cat with a long whip. The cat shook with fear and shrieked in pain.

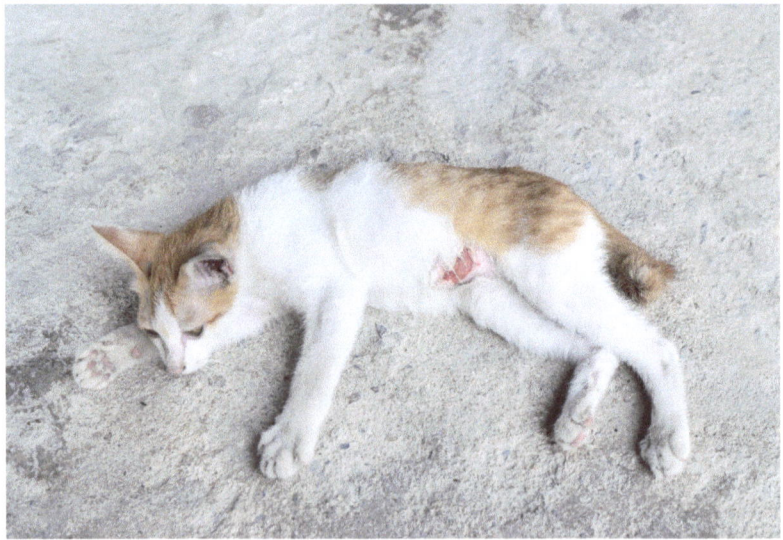

Vadim begged the peasant: "Please, don't beat the cat. I'll give you the last of my coins if you let him go."

"Certainly," the peasant smiled, taking the coins.

Again Vadim returned home without any bread, explaining: "I need still more money."

His father looked at him sadly. "Then, I must give you the last money we have."

On the way, Vadim said to himself: "I must be sure to buy some bread this time. We are both very hungry, and I cannot let my father starve."

But along the path, he saw a peasant in his yard kicking a snake.

At first, Vadim tried to keep walking. "It's only a snake," he thought.

But as he imagined the pain of the small, helpless snake, he felt overcome by sorrow.

"Even if it's just a snake, it's still being hurt," he thought, and went over to the peasant.

"Please, don't beat the snake," he begged. "I have only these last few coins. But I'll give them to you if you stop."

"Of course," said the peasant, taking his foot off the snake.

As Vadim watched the peasant walk off laughing, he put his hands in his empty pockets and thought to himself: "How can I have been so foolish to give away all my money again.. And I did this all for the life of a snake."

Vadim turned to go home, when the snake crawled over to him and tapped him on his foot with his tail. "Thank you," the snake told him: "You have saved my life and I am very grateful. So I will give you my magic ring."

The snake wriggled a few times, and the ring dropped on the ground at Vadim's feet.

Vadim picked it up, and the snake continued: "Wear this ring, and whenever you need anything, twist the ring on your finger, and say what you want to yourself. Then, you'll have it. If you need any more bread, tap your ring against a stone, and soon you will have plenty."

The snake wriggled off and disappeared into the grass.

Vadim returned home skipping and singing happily. When his father met him at the door, asking: "Have you finally brought back some bread?" Vadim replied excitedly.

"No. I have brought back something even better. Now we can have bread whenever we want. Look."

He thrust out his hand, as his father gasped. "Have you gone mad? Where can we get bread now? We have no more money."

In reply, Vadim bent down, tapped the ring against a stone, and wished: "May we now have bread."

Suddenly, a dozen loaves appeared before them. When Vadim tapped the ring again, a dozen more appeared.

The rest of that summer, Vadim and his father had bread and anything else they wanted – all with Vadim's twist of a ring and a wish. So awhile, they lived very happily. They had plenty of food, and in the fall, a good harvest.

Then, one winter morning, Vadim wondered what else the magic ring might do and said to himself: "I wish the trees near our house might have leaves of gold and diamonds."

At once, when he twisted the ring on his finger, all the leaves became leaves of gold and diamonds.

Everyone around the countryside began talking about the miraculous tress. People flocked from near and far to see them.

When the king of Latvia heard of this marvel, he came to see the trees for himself.

"How wondrous," he exclaimed, as Vadim showed him the golden trees.

After their tour, the king asked: "Can you come to my castle and turn my trees into diamonds and gold?"

"Gladly," Vadim agreed.

The next day, he mounted one of the king's horses and rode with him to his castle. After they arrived, Vadim walked around the garden twisting his magic ring. Soon all the leaves had turned into gold and diamonds.

"How marvelous," the king exclaimed. "Now to show my thanks, I want to send you home with the richest of treasures."

But before he could give Vadim anything, the queen, who had seen Vadim twist the ring on his finger, rode over to the king. She whispered the secret of the ring in his ear.

After she rode off, he turned to Vadim with a big smile:

"Please be my guest tonight in my castle. Tomorrow, I will send you home with the finest treasures."

But that night, as Vadim slept in a bed with silken sheets, the queen tiptoed in and slipped the ring off his finger.

In the morning, when Vadim woke up, he saw the ring was missing and hopped out of bed to search for it. When he glanced out the window, he noticed that all the gold and diamond leaves were gone. The trees were just ordinary trees again, for the ring had lost its magic powers, once it was taken from him.

Suddenly, a dozen soldiers burst through his door. They dragged him out of the room and took him before the king.

Angrily the king yelled at him. "You tricked me. You claimed you could turn my trees into gold and silver. But now all the gold and silver is gone. You are just a common swindler."

"No, no," Vadim sputtered, trying to explain about the missing ring. But the king told his soldiers: "Throw him in a dungeon. He will die by hanging tomorrow."

The soldiers dragged Vadim to a dark room in the cellar of the castle. As the heavy iron door slammed behind him, Vadim noticed a small window with thick wooden bars.

He sat down on a pile of straw, feeling doomed by the thick dungeon walls and heavy doors. Without the magic ring, there seemed no way out.

That night, the story of his plight spread through the countryside. Both they people and farmyard animals, spoke about Vadim's sad fate.

When the dog, mouse, and cat he had saved heard about his plight, they decided to help. Later that night, in the darkness, the mouse and cat snuck into the castle through a small hole in the wall. They crept into the bedchamber where the queen lay asleep with the ring in her mouth, afraid that someone might try to steal it as she slept.

In the moonlight, the mouse saw the ring glisten between her lips, and he crawled into her bed. Quietly, he slipped the tip of his tail into the ring and gave a little tug, which made the queen cough. The ring rolled out of her mouth and fell onto the floor.

The cat scooped the ring up in his teeth, ran out the door, and headed for the dungeon. As the cat arrived, the dog finished scratching a hole in the thick dungeon wall. The cat wriggled inside and saw Vadim sitting sadly in the corner.

Holding the ring in his mouth, he ran over to Vadim. When Vadim saw the ring, he grabbed it joyously.

"How marvelous," he exclaimed, slipping the ring back on his finger. He gave it a twist and wished aloud: "May I and my friends be out of the dungeon."

Instantly, the door opened, and he and the dog, cat, and mouse stepped into the cool night air. They walked through the castle and out the gate. He knew the king and queen could do nothing to him now, because he had the ring on his finger.

Once outside, he wished: "I want to be home again," and he was.

Thereafter, Vadim and his father lived happily in their house and had no more worries -- all because of the magic ring.

THE MOUNTAIN OF GEMS

An Adaptation of a Traditional Folk Tale from Turkmen

Aman lived with his old widowed mother in a small village in Turkmenia. They were very poor, because his mother had to support the family by herself. She cleaned the lambs' wool which shepherds brought to her, sold it to merchants to make rugs, and took in washing.

One day when Aman was old enough to work, his mother said to him:

"I can no longer work, my son. I don't have enough strength. Now you must find work and earn money to support us."

The next morning, Aman went out to look for work. He offered to help some shepherds tend their sheep.

He asked some rug merchants if he could weave their rugs. He spoke to some craftsmen making rings and bracelets.

But no one had any work for him.

When he came home each night, his mother sobbed: "Whatever will we do? How will we feed ourselves?"

So Aman knocked on many more doors and spoke to many more people. But nothing.

Finally, he came to the home of a rich noble, called a "bai." His house was shaped like a large canvas tent draped with cow hides.

Behind the house, many camels rested on the sand.

The bai came to the tent opening wearing his rainbow-striped robe. Aman asked as he had many times: "Do you have any work?"

The bai smiled broadly. "Yes," he said, pointing to the camels. "Tomorrow, I must go on a journey to seek gems, and I need someone to come with me."

"Certainly," Aman said.

The next morning, Aman appeared at the bai's tent, eager to begin work.

"Very good," said the bai. "Now, please kill a bull and skin it for me. Then, bring me four large sacks and a rug and get two camels ready to go on our journey."

"Gladly, master," said Aman.

After he killed and skinned one of the bulls, obtained a rug, and prepared the two camels, one camel carried the two large sacks and the bai mounted the other camel. With Aman walking beside him, they started off through the desert.

After several days, they arrived at the bottom of a mountain. The bai stopped the camels.

"Turn the rug inside out and lie down on it," he told Aman.

"How strange," Aman though, but afraid to disobey, he lay down on the rug.

As Aman lay there, the bai rolled up the rug around Aman like a big tube. He took a large piece of rope and tied it around the center of the bundle.

"I'll be back in a few minutes," said the bai.

The bai walked off and disappeared behind a nearby rock. Aman soon began to sweat under the hot desert sun.

"Whatever is my master doing?" he wondered.

Suddenly, two large black birds with bills like sharp swords and wings as large as a camel flew up. They were drawn by the smell of fresh meat from the newly killed bull.

They dove down, grabbed the rug with Aman in it, and flew away. Aman trembled with fear as the birds flew higher, yet trapped in the bundle of hides, he couldn't even move.

As the birds dropped the bundle on the mountain top, he felt a sharp bump. Then, he felt jabs of pain in his arms and legs as the birds pecked and clawed at the bundle.

Aman struggled to get out. Frightened by his thrashing, the birds screeched loudly and flew away.

Aman stood up, saw he was high on the mountain, and looked down on the bai below.

The bai waved his hands and shouted: "Good. You got there safely. Now please throw down the colored stones."

Aman looked down and saw the ground covered by hundreds of beautiful stones -- white diamonds, red rubies, blue sapphires, green emeralds. They glittered and sparkled in the sun.

Aman bent down and picked up the gems. He threw several handfuls down to the bai, who quickly scooped them up and put them in his sacks.

Suddenly, Aman stopped, feeling a chill of fear spread over him.

"How will I get down from here?" he asked the bai.

The bai laughed. "Oh, don't worry. Just throw down more stones until I fill these sacks. Then, I will tell you how to get down."

So Aman threw down more gems. At last, the sacks were full, and the bai put them on his camels' backs. He climbed on one of the camels.

"Now tell me how to get down," Aman cried.

The bai looked up and laughed heartily.

"Why should I tell you now? I have my gems. Look around, and you will see those who worked for me before. They were all fools like you."

With that, the bai rode away.

Aman shook with terror. He was all alone and all around were white bones and skulls of the men who had once worked for the bai.

Frantically, he searched for a way to climb down, walking through the piles of bones and skulls. But the mountain was very steep and jagged, and he could find no path.

Aman sank down on his knees sobbing.

"Oh, no. No. Is this what will become of me?"

Suddenly, as he sobbed, there was a rush of wings overhead. A large eagle landed on his back and began pecking at him. Then, rising up, it stretched out its large claws to grab Aman and take him to its nest.

Aman leaped to his feet and ran. But the eagle kept coming at him, its large claws reaching out like hooks.

Terrified, Aman stared at the claws coming closer, about to grab him, when he had an idea. He reached out and grabbed the eagle's legs with both hands.

As he held on tightly, the eagle shrieked loudly, rose up into the air, and flew in circles, flapping its wings and shaking its legs. Around and around it went, trying to shake off Aman, but he kept holding on.

Tiring, the eagle flew lower and lower. When it came close to the ground, Aman let go and dropped back onto the sand.

As the eagle flew away, Aman cried joyously: "I'm safe. I've been spared from a certain and terrible death."

Aman headed back to the village to look for work again. Soon he was in the marketplace and stopped in several shops.

"Have you any work?" he asked. But nothing.

As he was about to enter a small grocery store, he saw the bai striding along, leading his camels. On their saddles hung golden statues, colorful tapestries, and ornaments the bai had bought with the gems from the mountain.

The bai walked past Aman without recognizing him. Aman turned and caught up to the bai.

"Do you have any work?" Aman asked.

"Why, yes," said the bai, still not recognizing Aman. "Come home with me, and I will have work for you tomorrow."

As the day dawned, the bai told Aman, as before: "I am going on a journey to get gems."

As before, he asked Aman to kill a bull, skin it, prepare two camels, and bring four sacks and a rug. Again Aman did so.

After Aman loaded the skin, four sacks, and the rug onto one of the camels, they began their journey to the same mountain. The bai rode on one camel, while Aman walked beside the other with the bull's hide, four sacks, and rug.

At the mountain, the bai told Aman: "Lie down on the rug and wrap yourself in it."

Aman looked at the bai with a puzzled frown.

"I don't understand. Can you show me how?"

"Fool," the bai said with a scowl. "What can't you understand? What I have asked is very simple. I will show you."

The bai lay down on the rug. At once, Aman grabbed the coiled rope from the camel's saddle and rolled up the rug with the bai inside it. He strapped the rope tightly around the bundle.

"Let me out," cried the bai, pounding his fists against the side of the bundle.

But before he could say more, two huge black birds with large wings and sharp claws flew up.

They grabbed the rug with the bai in it and flew to the top of the mountain. Then, they dropped the bundle on the ground and began tearing it apart with their beaks and claws.

Inside, the bai thrashed his arms and feet about, kicking and yelling. He thrashed so wildly that he scared the black birds and they flew away.

As the bai stood up, Aman yelled up to him: "Now, bai, you can throw the gems down to me as I did for you."

Suddenly, the bai recognized Aman and began shaking with fear.

"How did you get down from the mountain?" he cried out.

Aman replied with a laugh: "Just throw down some more gems. When I have filled up these sacks, I will tell you how."

The bai threw down more gems, and Aman quickly picked them up and put them in the sacks. Soon the sacks were bulging with gems, and he tied them onto the camels' backs.

"Now tell me know to get down," cried the bai.

But Aman only laughed scornfully. "Look around you bai," he said. "You'll see the bones of your past workers everywhere. Why don't you ask them how to get down?"

Aman turned and headed home riding one camel and leading the other, which was carrying the bulging sacks. He whistled happily as he rode.

"Won't my mother be pleased when she sees all these gems?" he thought. "Now I can give her what I have earned for my work."

As for the bai...He is still on the mountain top with the rest of his workers.

ABOUT THE AUTHOR

Gini Graham Scott has published over 50 books with mainstream publishers, focusing on social trends, work and business relationships, and personal and professional development. Some of these books include *The Very Next New Thing*, *The Talk Show Revolution*, *The Privacy Revolution*, *The Battle for Personal Privacy*, and *Fantasy Worlds*.

She has gained extensive media interest for previous books, including appearances on *Good Morning America*, *Oprah*, *Montel Williams*, *CNN*, and hundreds of radio interviews. She has frequently been quoted by the media and has set up websites to promote her most recent books at www.ginigrahamscott.com and www.changemakerspublishingandwriting..com. As of this writing, she has about 75,000 listings in Google Search Results.

She has become a regular Huffington Post blogger since December 2012, and has a Facebook page featuring her books and films at www.facebook.com/changemakerspublishing.

She has written, produced, and sometimes directed over 60 short videos, which are featured on her Changemakers Productions website at www.changemakersproductions.com and on YouTube at www.youtube.com/changemakersprod.

Her screenplays, mostly in the drama, crime, legal thriller, and sci-fi genres, include several that consider the social implications of science and technological breakthroughs and changes in society, including *The New Child, New Identity, Dead No More, Tax Revolt,* and *The Suicide Party.* All of these are in development with trailers, business plans, and interested directors and talent.

She has a PhD in sociology from U.C. Berkeley and MAs in anthropology, pop culture and lifestyles, recreation and tourism, and organizational/consumer/audience behavior from Cal State, East Bay. She is getting an MA in communications in June 2016.

She is also the Creative Director of Publishers, Agents and Films (www.publishersagentsandfilms.com), a service which connects writers to publishers, agents, and the film industry.

Her feature film, SUICIDE PARTY: SAVE DAVE, which she wrote and executive produced, is being released in the summer of 2015. Details are at www.suicidepartyfilm.com.

Additional bio and promotional material is at her websites at www.ginigrahamscott.com and www.changemakerspublishingandwriting.com.